A WINTERFOLD CHRISTMAS

by Harriet Evans

© Harriet Evans 2015
Published by Venetia Books

Illustrations and design by Sarah Lawrence

A Winterfold Christmas is a short but sweet festive story from *Sunday Times* bestselling author Harriet Evans.

When chef Joe Thorne rashly promises to cook Christmas dinner for his girlfriend Cat's family, little does he know what he's letting himself in for... At Winterfold, their beautiful rambling house in the heart of the English countryside, things have always been done a certain way and Martha Winter, matriarch of the clan, knows what she wants. Still reeling from her husband's death and the loss of her perfect family, is Martha ready to enjoy Christmas? Will the Winter family be able to come together one more time?

Packed with recipes for you to try, favourite carols and Christmas memories, A Winterfold Christmas is a festive story to warm the heart.

Joe

November 2014

'I've never cooked a Christmas meal before, no. I don't understand what all the fuss is about, to be honest.'

Sheila Cowper, Joe's boss, stopped in the act of pouring a glass of wine, her mouth open. 'What's that now?'

'I've never cooked a Christmas meal before.' Joe Thorne shifted under her appalled gaze. 'Come on, it's not that big a deal. It's November. I've got ages, haven't I?'

'You're joking, aren't you? You? Never cooked Christmas? And you've offered to do the cooking . . .' Sheila hugged herself, eyes dancing, 'at *Winterfold?* You've taken over from . . . from *Martha Winter* and you've never done a Christmas meal before?' She shivered. 'Ooh, this is great.'

Joe scratched his neck where the label of his chef's whites always itched. Trying not to sound arrogant, he said, 'Sheila, I am a professional chef, you know.'

'Ha-ha!' Sheila was laughing. 'Oh, I know, love. Now listen, don't get me wrong.' She leaned on the bar. 'Bob? *Bob?* she called out. 'Come over yere! Joe's saying he's never cooked a Christmas meal before!'

Bob, their oldest regular, whose age was a matter of fierce debate in the village, cupped one ear with his hand. 'He *what?*'

'He's never cooked a Christmas meal before!'

'But ain't he cooking furr them up there at Winterfold, instead of Mrs Winter?' he said. 'Susan told me as he was. You sure about that, my dear?'

Sheila laughed, jerking her head in Joe's direction.

'Well, well,' said Bob, gazing reproachfully at Joe. 'That's very interesting. Very interesting indeed. Tell me, do you know how she makes her bread sauce? Do you?'

'No,' said Joe. 'I've . . . I mean, I've made bread sauce, OK?' He wished he didn't sound so defensive.

'Sure you have, dear,' said Sheila. 'I've eaten it. It's delicious. Everything you make's delicious, Joe.' She tapped the blackboard above the Oak's gleaming bar. 'Why do you think we got people booking seven months in advance to eat here? But you're not Martha Winter, my love.'

'I'm not saying I am,' said Joe, nettled.

'I'm just . . . well, you're a brave man, that's all.'

'How?' said Joe, though he knew the answer.

'Taking on the Winters at Christmas,' came the reply. 'There's no one does Christmas better than Martha. I can't believe she agreed to let you do the Christmas meal. It's legendary. You know, one year, she cooked the potatoes three times, to get them right?' She ticked them off on her fingers. 'Boiled, shaken around in rice flour and polenta, lightly fried in olive oil, *then* in the hot oven with the goose fat. You know once,' said Sheila, warming to her theme, 'once, she cooked a chicken *inside a goose*. And, *and* a turkey as well. And she did it all running that house and raising three children, as well as looking after David and having a hundred people turning up to the drinks party, too. Oh, she even read the lesson at the Nine Lessons. "The people that walked in darkness have seen a great light," said Sheila with relish. 'That's her. She reads beautifully, you know.'

'Well, things are—' Joe began.

But Sheila interrupted. 'She always looked so nice, too. Not that she doesn't now, of course.' She stopped in the act of pouring a second glass. 'I do hope she's all right, poor Martha. Does she seem all right to you?'

'Martha? She's fine. This time of year's difficult, of course.' They nodded at each other.

For years the Winters had been thought of unofficially as the first family of the village – though they would have been horrified at such a description. But people loved David, the cartoonist creator of Wilbur the dog, beloved around the world. Martha was the businesslike one, the one who remembered birthdays and made lasagnes for sick people, and David was the kind, charming one, who kissed children and loved singing show tunes. Their three children had long since grown up, of course, but they still – all of them – had thought of Winterfold as home.

Then, two years ago, disaster struck. David had a heart attack in the middle of a family lunch and died. Things had moved on, though – that's what everyone said, anyway. But in fact, they hadn't for Martha.

'You need to make sure your mother-in-law's OK,' said Sheila, whipping him with a tea towel.

'She's my grandmother-in-living-together,' pointed out Joe. 'Cat and I aren't married. And she's her granddaughter.'

'You know what I mean. Martha needs looking after. She pretends she doesn't but she does. After last year, too . . .' Sheila's face darkened. 'Oh dear.'

'Look, Sheila, I know Barbados was a disaster.' He rubbed his forehead, as though instantly sweating at the memory of last year's attempt to have a family Christmas not at Winterfold. 'But things are different at Winterfold now. I'm there. Cat and I are together. We've each got Luke and Jamie. It's time for Martha and Cat to take it easy. They've got me. I can look after them.'

He wished he felt as certain as he sounded.

'Oh, I know it all,' said Sheila, and she smiled at him and put the glasses on a tray along with some roasted nuts tossed in fennel seeds and sea salt. 'They're the luckiest women west of London, those Winter girls. But you'd better not screw it up, my love. They take Christmas seriously up there.'

Joe thought of Cat, at this very moment stalking the hedgerows on this chilly, damp November afternoon picking sloes to make sloe gin, a reluctant Luke by her side. 'Tell me about it,' he said.

When he came to think about it, he had absolutely no memory of how he'd decided to offer to do Christmas, and in such a peremptory fashion. It was unlike him. Joe was a planner – careful, shy. It was what he had in common with Cat: they were introverts, not crazy arm-waving extroverts like Cat's cousin Lucy, who talked nineteen to the dozen, or Cat's aunt Florence, who frequently walked into door frames because she was waving her arms around too much.

'I'll do it,' he'd announced one morning, a couple of weeks ago, when it was still October, Halloween hadn't even happened and Christmas seemed an age away. Martha had idly mentioned it at breakfast and he'd leaped right in there.

'We're here for the first time. Together.'

'Is Jamie coming?' Cat looked up. 'I thought he was with Jemma.'

'He is with her.' Jamie was Joe's son from a previous relationship. He didn't want to admit to anyone, especially Cat, that he hoped by doing all of the Christmas cooking to distract himself from the hole in his heart when his son wasn't around on days like these. He saw him little enough as it was. He couldn't bear to think about how much he missed Jamie. 'But we'll see him in the New Year.' He smiled at Cat, lovingly. 'Point is, this should be special. Let me do it. The meal, some drinks the night before, the mince pies and the cake.' He waved a gracious hand around. 'It's not right you should have to do all the work.'

'No,' Martha had said, amused, in that clear, slightly scary way she had. 'No, I don't mind the work. You could help me. You don't have to do it all.'

He should have just agreed. It'd have been so much better.

'No, Martha. I've been thinking about it . . .' He hadn't been thinking about it that he knew of. It hadn't crossed his mind! 'It's time you relaxed. What kind of chef am I – and what kind of

8

partner to Cat – if I can't knock up a decent Christmas meal? You know, Barbados wasn't quite right for us . . .'

Across the table, Cat shuddered and gave a grimace.

'Now we're all here, I'd like to do it. Show you all it's my home as well, and that I'm the man who can do all that, sort it all out. You know, prove myself to you. Show you that I'm . . .' He trailed off, suddenly aware this had escalated from being a casual conversation into some Russell-Crowe-in-*Gladiator*-style declaration of intent. 'Would that be OK with you all?'

Martha had simply shrugged. Luke had looked at Joe curiously, but Cat met his gaze, her eyes filmy with tears. Tough, hard Cat, who never showed emotion, his beautiful willowy girl who made his heart leap every morning when he woke up and looked at her, lying next to him. He had made a vow to himself that she'd never feel afraid or lonely again. He would let her fly, mend her broken wings . . . though when he said stuff like that she made vomiting noises and hooted with laughter. She was tough, like her grandmother.

But he'd got to her now, he'd made her cry. Joe's heart swelled.

'We'll have beef,' he said, thumping the table. 'And three kinds of potatoes. And the Brussels sprouts will taste like heaven. I'll make the mince pies, the sausage rolls—'

Luke, Cat's son, who was munching away at a bowl of Shreddies, looked up. 'You make the best sausage rolls in the world, Joe,' he said briefly, then went back to his cereal.

'Thanks, Luke!' Joe felt a swell of gratification. 'Thanks, buddy. Sausage rolls, um . . . the Christmas cake, the Christmas log – I'll do a ham for Boxing Day, and roast a turkey just in case we need some extra cold meats.' He reached into his pocket for the tiny notebook that was always on his person. 'Bread sauce infused with cranberries, how about that?'

There was a pause.

Cat said, delicately, 'Lucy doesn't eat beef.'

'Oh. OK, fine!' Joe scribbled this down.

'I loathe cranberries,' said Martha. 'They're American, apart from anything else. Like English muffins. We don't eat cranberries.'

We don't eat cranberries. 'Eggnog?'

'I like eggnog when I want to catch salmonella and nearly die. Raw eggs, Joe. Bad idea.'

'Oh.' Undaunted, Joe carried on scribbling.

'Listen, if you're sure you want to, then by all means. It's very kind of you.' Martha stood up. 'I'd better go and do some work. They want the revises by lunchtime. This is wonderful news. If you're sure you want to.'

'I'm absolutely sure.'

'As long as you don't blow the fuse box like you did when you cooked for Cat's birthday.'

Joe smiled, patiently. 'Ha-ha,' he said. 'I think that's the electrics, not me.'

'It's never happened before,' Martha told him, and he felt the tiny licking flames of irritation being stoked inside him. 'You switch the kettle on too much, that's the trouble. The electrics at Winterfold are fine.'

'OK, I'm sure it's me.' Joe bowed. 'I won't blow the fuse box. Thank you, Martha.'

'You sure it's OK, Gran?' said Cat, catching hold of Martha's hand as she passed by.

'Absolutely,' said Martha flatly. 'I'm not really looking forward to Christmas. This makes it easier.'

'Why aren't you looking forward to it?' said Cat, troubled.

Martha shook her head. 'Nothing you can help with, darling. I'm fine. Just . . . more memories than usual this year, that's all. Ones that I don't want to leave me.'

'Oh, Gran. What kind of memories? Southpaw?'

But Martha ignored the question. 'I must get on.' She patted Joe on the back. 'Well, Joseph. The baton passes. Good luck, my boy.'

Joe thought he caught a twinkle in her eye as she walked off, but he wasn't sure.

JOE'S SECRET BEST SAUSAGE ROLLS
IN THE ENTIRE WORLD

Makes 30-40 *mini sausage rolls*

2 rolls of ready-rolled puff pastry (ideally the all-butter variety, not the stuff made with oil, thoroughly defrosted if frozen)

15–20 good quality chipolatas depending on size

small bunch of thyme that has dried out over previous two weeks (sounds fiddly but is absolutely worth it I promise you)

100g parmesan, grated finely (may need more)

black pepper, grated

beaten egg and a little milk to loosen

Preheat the oven to 220°C/Fan 200°C/Gas 7. Carefully, so that you don't crack it, roll out the puff pastry flat, landscape-style.

Put two sausages end to end, vertically squashing them together at the tips. Scatter dried thyme and lots of parmesan down one side of each sausage, packing it in. Add some freshly ground pepper.

Cut the pastry and pinch together to form a little seal. You will judge best at what width to cut but don't waste pastry, you only need a small overhang. Ideally you can fit four–five lengths on one roll.

Repeat along the puff pastry until it is all used up, then cut using kitchen scissors (much better than a knife for this task) into small sausage rolls, no longer than 1 inch.

Brush with beaten egg and milk. Cook for 12–14 minutes on a greased baking tray in the preheated oven, or until golden brown and crispy and delicious-looking

Tip: Can be frozen before cooking after cutting.

Cat

Cat Winter hated Christmas. She loved late autumn, the country-side releasing its frantic hold on life and sinking into black and grey stark beauty. Releasing her hand from her five-year-old son's, Cat tied her hair back and rammed the woollen hat over her head, as Luke tramped alongside her, complaining.

'Maman! Why on *earth* do we have to do this?'

Cat hid a smile. 'Because sloe-hunting's fun.'

'It's not fun. I had to go collecting sloes last week with Joe and Jamie for the Oak. I didn't like it then. Plus I just pricked my finger again. It's so *dangerous*.'

'Oh, *chéri*.' Cat chucked him under the chin. 'Don't make such a blooming fuss.'

'I'm not.' Luke crossed his arms and stood stock-still in the middle of the muddy path. 'You said it'd be fun last year and my thumb got infected from that thorn. It was *green*. I want to go home.'

Cat always thought you could tell her son was French when it came to matters of his own health, about which he was deeply concerned, she being more of the 'if it drops off then we'll worry' school.

'If you help me I'll let you choose a chocolate from Gran's chocolate selection when we get back,' said Cat, resorting to bribery and hating herself.

'OK,' Luke said, happily. 'Thanks, Maman.'

On the fields above Winterfold the final autumn colour was almost indecent: the trees in the woodland behind wore every shade from crayfish pink to fluorescent yellow, with green, ochre, brown and coral in between. Ahead of them, the setting sun cast rosy-gold ripples across the grey-blue skies.

The hedgerows ahead of them were almost bare now, black-blue twigs flecked with phosphorescent lichen. The afternoon was utterly still; it was the first weekend after the clocks had gone back, and most folk were probably inside, safe from the sudden chill. Cat shivered; it would be Christmas soon, and she felt uneasy. Something was troubling her, in the back of her mind. She couldn't work out what. She shook her head, shaking out the negative thoughts.

'Where shall we go?' she said to Luke.

'This way,' he said. 'There were loads here last week.'

'Oh, good idea. You see, you are a good sloe-hunter.' But when they got to the corner of the field the branches were bare. Cat stared around in dismay.

'I'm sure most of the birds have had them,' she said brightly, but inwardly she seethed. *Other sloe-pickers, more like.*

Simon Ollerenshaw, husband of the local vicar, Kathy, was a real forager, hunting tirelessly all year round for food in the hedge-rows and fields around Winter Stoke. He liked his sloes, Cat knew: Simon could leave an entire hedgerow bare. She wouldn't have put it past him to have snaffled the whole lot. Village feelings ran high around sloe-picking time.

She could recall so clearly the years of sloe-hunting with her grandfather David who, before his arthritis got too bad, had the most agile and precise fingers. He could delve past the hard, firm bar of the thorny branch, dodging its pricks, and pluck the juiciest, plumpest sloes from the centre of the bush. The ones almost the size of a ten-pence coin, sleek and black, brushed with navy-purple and chalky colouring.

'Ha-ha! Bingo!' he'd shout, in childish delight. And the smell – that unmistakable scent of sharp, sallow fruitfulness that was, for her, Christmas at Winterfold. Before the miserable years in Paris, before she lost herself.

Since she'd been back in England, she had been happy almost every day – as happy as she could ever feel, since something inside her was broken now and would never entirely mend. But Christmas was what brought that bleakness to the fore and was the reason they had spent the money last year on the disastrous holiday to Barbados. The holiday seemed to symbolise the time of sadness in Paris: the tiny tree, not much taller than her upright hand, which she'd put up in Madame Poulain's flat, only to have it thrown away – 'No, Catherine, no plants inside, on my carpet' – the sight on the TV news of shopping in London; the carols you'd hear in Marks and Spencer; the view, once, on the front of a free newspaper, of Bath Abbey with the Christmas tree outside, the lights, the happy busyness of the place; and her, alone in the tiny *chambre de bonne* with a fitfully slumbering Luke on Christmas Eve, staring out at the black night sky and wondering what they were doing now, over in England, at Winterfold.

She recalled it all, in pinpoint-precise detail. She had been the only child there for years, brought up by her grandparents after her mother left, and it was an often lonely existence. So Christmas was like an explosion of family and colour and food. Her cousin Lucy's obsession with Christmas, the award ceremonies for best presents, best Christmas outfit, best singing along with the carol singers who serenaded them on Christmas Eve. The new bottle of Baileys, Southpaw's Rat Pack Christmas album, Martha's gingerbread, the Christmas drinks party every year at Winterfold.

Now she was safe, secure, happy – and she had Joe, too – yet Christmas was the one thing Cat still hadn't learned to enjoy.

'Is Lucy coming for Christmas?' Luke said, breaking into her train of thought. 'Here. Look, over there.'

'Oh, you're brilliant,' said Cat, gratefully, as she spotted the grey-green leaves, the chalky-black berries. She spread open the old cloth bag still kept in Southpaw's study to collect the sloes in. 'Why don't you hold the bag open? I'll pick. Not sure. Lucy's being vague as usual.' She bit her tongue; Luke noticed everything, and she didn't want him asking Lucy what that meant. 'She has a new flatmate. She might spend Christmas with him. He's called Orlando. She likes him a lot.'

'A new flatmate? What does that mean?' said Luke, solemnly holding the bag open as wide as he could.

'Irene moved out. She used to live in the flat. Now Orlando's moved in.'

'Is he her boyfriend?' Luke was very keen on Lucy. He'd stand and stare at her and then timidly climb on to her lap, only for Lucy to exclaim with joy and kiss him repeatedly, at which point he'd immediately scurry off into the corner and stand there staring at her again.

'No idea.' Cat had had a conversation with her cousin the previous day which was inconclusive in almost every respect.

Was she coming for Christmas? She didn't know. Did she know what was up with Gran? No, but she thought she might if she thought about it. Could she get Cat a discount at a garden centre that advertised with *Country Matters*, the magazine she worked for? Perhaps. Was she going out with this Orlando bloke? No, not really, but they sort of cohabited as if they were man and wife and . . .

'I'm not sure, darling. She wasn't really sure of her plans. It's still only November.'

'It'd be nice if she had a boyfriend. Like you have Joe.'

'It would, but – ow!' Cat had reached towards a particularly gnarly patch, catching her finger on a long, tricksy thorn. She sucked the gloved finger, looked around and realised it was suddenly almost dark. 'We should go soon.'

'I like living here with you and Joe and Jamie,' said Luke.

'Well, I do, too,' said Cat. She put the handful of sloes into his bag and gave him a quick kiss.

'Can you ring Lucy again and ask her to come for Christmas here, pleeease?'

'Yes, Luke,' said Cat. 'OK, then. What about Aunt Florence?'

Luke shook his head. Florence scared him. She'd once hidden in a cupboard and jumped out at him yelling 'PIRATE ATTACK!' and this had totally freaked him out for days. Unfortunately, he still remembered it. When Cat's aunt had been over from Italy for Easter, Luke had been the one who'd hidden himself away in his room, for hours on end.

Cat smiled at the memory and then she straightened up, alert as a meerkat. 'Look, little one!' she said, pointing. 'A whole load of them! Bingo! Quick!'

'Why are you whispering?' said Luke. 'There's no one else around.'

'You can't be too sure,' Cat hissed.

They walked briskly to the corner of the field, by the stile that led down to the lane, where shade and light had conspired to multiply the crop of sloes which somehow had not been disturbed, by man or beast.

The shadows were lengthening.

'Come on,' said Cat. 'Let's work fast. Then we can go home and have fish finger sandwiches by the fire and watch *The Princess Bride*. How does that sound?'

'Can we not watch the Rodents of Unusual Size?' asked Luke.

'Yes, we'll fast forward it.'

'Good!' said Luke, enthusiastically.

Together they began picking, nimble fingers plucking two, three at a time, and they sang carols as they went. Like all the Winters, they loved singing, and Cat, who had a lovely voice, sang here now, when previously she hadn't. She hoped her grandfather was watching them, and that he approved, approved of it all.

> The holly and the ivy,
> When they are both full grown,
> Of all the trees that are in the wood,
> The holly bears the crown!
> *O, the rising of the sun,*
> *And the running of the deer,*

The playing of the merry organ,
Sweet singing in the choir!

'I'm excited about Christmas,' said Luke. 'I think it's going to be great. Better than in Paris.'

'Do you remember living in France?' said Cat, curiously.

Luke breathed out hard, ruffling his thick dark fringe. He needed a haircut, though she hated how grown-up he looked when his hair was newly shorn.

'Sometimes. I remember Madame Poulain screaming at me. And the climbing frame in the park across the bridge from our apartment.'

'Jardin Albert Schweitzer,' said Cat, automatically.

'And the compotes . . .' Luke paused. 'We don't eat compote much, these days.'

She laughed. 'No, we don't, do we?'

'I'm glad we moved to here.'

'Me too,' said Cat, throwing her arm around him. 'Oh, darling, me too.'

As they crossed the field, scant pickings swinging by her side in the cloth bag, Cat reflected that Christmas might not be so bad after all. She churned the thought around in her mind, wondering again why she still felt uneasy. Why something was amiss. As she locked the gate and held Luke's arm to wait for a car to pass them in the lane, it suddenly occurred to her, like remembering a smell or colour: Gran. Someone crying in the night. The vague sense of something being wrong. Something was up with Gran, she knew it. She didn't know why, though.

DAVID WINTER'S SLOE GIN

From October onwards the hedgerows, lanes and byways are brimming full of sloes. Collect as many as you can; we call it sloe-hunting. Enlist young fingers and sharp eyes if you can. My granddaughter Catherine comes up to my hip and is a ferocious sloe-hunter.

I put all the sloes I've managed to gather in with a litre of gin. A screwtop bottle is not ideal here; I use a Kilner or preserving jar (something that doesn't leak when turned upside down).

There is great controversy over whether to put the sugar in at the start (about 250g per litre) or after it's been steeping for a few weeks. I say leave the sugar out as long as you can, but others – including my darling wife – disagree. The crucial thing is, every morning, to turn the jar upside down several times. I do this whilst humming the opening bars of *Night and Day* by Frank Sinatra; you may pick the tune you prefer. Da-de-da-da-da-de-da-da-da.

If we lived in an ideal world, one would let the sloes steep for three months, then add the sugar, turning firmly again, and bottle ready for drinking at Christmas. But picking them in late October when they are ripe means about eight weeks only if you want the gin to be ready for Christmas that year, rather than waiting patiently for the next. As I say, if one lived in an ideal world one would not have drunk it all the previous Christmas, but what use is sloe gin in June? I find eight weeks to be sufficient, if not ideal. It is the season of goodwill, after all.

An excellent cocktail can be made using one part sloe gin to 3 parts Prosecco or Champagne. This is known as The Harry for reasons now lost in the mists of time. Beware of serving your guests more than two Harrys. As they say of Martinis, they are like breasts: one is not enough, three is too many.

Florence

December

'So, Lucy!' Florence beamed at her niece over a menu. 'What will you have? I must say, I love Peruvian food. Isn't this place wonderful?'

She watched as her niece looked doubtfully around the restaurant at the other single customer pushing what looked like tar round his plate, at the waiter dolefully polishing a shiny plate decorated with faint flowers whilst staring into space. A hairy, loud fly dramatically flung itself repeatedly at the glass frontage, desperate to escape.

'Er . . . yeah. Wonderful,' said Lucy who, being under thirty and living in Dalston, was fully conversant with Peruvian food and knew of two much better Peruvian restaurants nearby.

'I know it doesn't seem much but it's great, honestly.' Florence held the menu up and scanned it intently and thoroughly. 'I brought Jim here, and he loved it.' She scrutinised the choice of dishes. 'Mmmm . . . well, the ceviche for me, I think. What about you?'

Lucy put the menu down. 'I'm not that hungry. I'll just have some rice.'

Florence stared at her niece in consternation. 'Lucy, what's wrong with you? You normally eat like a . . . like a . . .' Florence trailed off, frowning at herself.

'Like a horse? A platoon of hungry troops? An army of cockroaches?' Lucy smiled, weakly. 'I'm just not feeling like food.'

'What's up?'

'Oh . . .' Lucy wound a skein of fine hair around one finger. 'Problems . . . problems with . . . oh Lord. I don't know how you say it.'

'Lucy!' cried Florence, alarmed, looking at her niece's pale face, the grey circles under her eyes, hearing her flat tone. 'Darling, what's up?'

'It's nothing really serious.' She smiled again. 'Don't look so aghast, Aunt Flo. Merely problems in love. Gosh. That sounds so yucksome. I'm in love with my flatmate, is the long and short of it.'

'Ah.' Florence put her arms over her menu and leaned forwards, thrilled to think she might be of help to her younger niece, of whom she was inordinately fond. 'Well, that's wonderful, Lucy. It's a hard path, a love like that, even today when we think equality is closer than ever before. I applaud you.' She took Lucy's hands, trying to conceal the deep surprise she felt, especially at Lucy's choice: a particularly uninspiring young woman to Florence's mind. But then, what did she know about the mysteries of sapphic love? 'Brava, to the both of you, you and . . . Irene, was it? Forgive me – I'm so bad with names.'

'Aunt Flo!' Lucy pulled her hands away. 'Not Irene! I'm not gay, Flo. And if I was – good grief, no way. Irene moved out, thank God. She was awful, and Chairman Miaow was just the worst.'

'Chairman who?'

'Her cat. He was called Chairman Miaow,' said Lucy with a blank expression. 'He had extremely disturbed guts. Living with him was an utter trial. No, it's not Irene. It's . . . Orlando.' She lengthened the vowels. 'He's new. He's only been living with me for four weeks. Four weeks! He comes from Worcestershire. He grew up on a farm. He works on the magazine with me.'

'Oh, how wonderful. So you work together and live together. That's lovely. What does he do on *Country Life*?'

'*Country Matters*, Aunt Flo. We're the poor man's *Country Life*. We're its slightly chavvy cousin. We have ads for Ronseal and L'Oréal, not sales of pictures of horses at Sotheby's.'

'But you're liking it still?' said Florence.

'Oh, it's just bliss after the *Daily News*. No one monitoring whether I've got any CC cream and what my views on jumpsuits are . . .'

Florence felt, as she sometimes did with Lucy, that she was speaking a dialect, a version of English that she didn't quite understand.

'I love all that countryside stuff, and these sweet letters we get from readers and people telling us things – I'm writing a feature on rook pie at the moment for March. I've interviewed a man who broke his back in three places climbing up into a rookery to get at the young birds.'

Florence made a face. 'Sounds grim, darling. Poor things.'

'They live a happier life than the pigs who give you bacon, or the chickens you blithely eat who've never seen daylight and can't move,' said Lucy, briskly.

Florence nodded, chastened. 'Of course, of course. Tell me about Orlando, though. Go on. Stop changing the subject.'

'Oh, it's just hopeless, that's why. He's . . . he's got thick, crazy hair and he's so shy and weird!' Lucy clasped her hands together, rapturously. 'And he doesn't understand London and he's really lonely and I – I . . .' She trailed off. 'Never mind. I sound like a loon. But oh, Aunt Flo, I was such a baby with Tom, and all the others. This feels different. We're so – when I'm with him, I just *get* him. Finally, I *get* someone and what they want. Without either of us even having to *speak*,' she ended, dramatically.

'Have you told him any of this?' said Florence, with a sympathetic pang of recognition.

'No, no.' Lucy shook her head, and looked mortified. 'It'd ruin everything. He's very private. Plus, we're flatmates. It's just – I want to run my hands through his hair so much, *plus* I really want to snog him. And I'm terrified one day I'll get pissed and creep into his room and assault him or something—'

She stopped, instantly blushing red, as the waiter appeared and licked his pencil sadly, in a manner that privately delighted her aunt.

Florence looked up. 'Hello. The ceviche, please. And the prawns.'

'There is no prawns,' said the waiter, flatly. 'We can do battered octopus. That is what we have today.'

'Oh.' Florence was disconcerted. She shrugged. 'Fine. Bring whatever's best. I leave it to you!' She handed him the menus with a flourish.

'A good choice,' said the waiter sadly, and bowed, so that the tiny bells on his waistcoat jangled.

'Jingle bells,' said Lucy, as he retreated. They smiled at each other. 'Oh, and that's the other thing. Christmas. Orlando is spending Christmas on his own. In London.' She looked out of the window, at the traffic speeding down the anonymous North London road. 'How grim. Just him alone with a cracker, and no one else.' Her eyes filled with tears. 'I can't decide whether I should just stay with him. Say my family's in Barbados again—'

Florence shuddered. 'Never again.'

'Oh God, no,' agreed Lucy.

'Darling Luce,' said Florence, 'you can't stay with this boy at Christmas. Think how much we'd miss you! He wouldn't ask that of you.'

'He wouldn't, no, but perhaps I should. He says no one in his family wants him for Christmas, and he's better off staying there. His family sounds awful. His dad actually *told* Orlando he wished he wasn't his son. And his brother, he lent him some money, and he never paid it back. And Orlando is so clever and bright they hate him for not wanting to work on the farm. And he doesn't like London, he's like a lost soul in a tweed jacket and wellies wandering around Dalston. Oh, it's so sad!'

Florence decided, privately, that Orlando sounded like the kind of man who might well be asked to spend Christmas alone. She said, brightly, 'Well, we shall miss you a great deal if you don't come back. What will I do without you to read with me?'

They had a tradition, the two of them both bookworms, of

rereading an old Christmas classic each year. Last Christmas, in the sweltering heat of Barbados, both of them had reread *The Pickwick Papers* – the Christmas section – dreaming of English lanes piled high with snow, heavy laden tables, jolly friends and roaring log fires.

But Lucy shrugged. 'I don't know, Flo. We have to face up to the fact we won't always go to Winterfold for Christmas.'

Florence swallowed. 'I know, darling. But it makes me awfully sad, to think of you all on your own in London while we're all enjoying Joe's Christmas lunch.'

'Joe's doing Christmas lunch?' Lucy's eyes widened. 'Oh, but that's major. What does Gran say?'

Florence shrugged. 'Not much. She said it was fine when I saw her.'

'When did you see her?'

The fly buzzed louder than ever next to Florence. She batted it away.

'Last week. She came down for the Gothic Imagination exhibition and we had tea. Jim said he thought she looked rather peaky, but this time of year – it's always hard for her.'

'We'll see.' Lucy put on a brave face. 'How's work?'

'Great. I'm doing a Christmas lecture on nativity scenes in Renaissance art at the National Gallery later this month.' Florence rubbed her hands together. 'Should be wonderful, but I'm rather nervous about it. Do come. It's on Friday 19th December, I think.' She looked over. 'Oh, marvellous! This looks delicious.'

The waiter put three plates down: some greens, something black, and a dish full of red peppers.

'Lucy, is your stomach rumbling?'

'Perhaps,' said Lucy. 'I bet your lectures will be wonderful, Flo. You always were the best aunt.'

'Well, not much competition.'

'No, but you were. The best person to read stories and play with us, and explain things. Oh, you always explained everything so well! About history and people. And at Christmas reading me and Cat *Narnia* and . . .' Lucy trailed off. 'Oh dear. I think I'd better come home for Christmas. I'll be too miserable in London, thinking of you all there having a wonderful time.'

'Well, I think that's the right decision,' said Florence, happily. She blew her niece a kiss, nearly knocking over her water glass. 'I'm looking forward to Joe's attempt at Christmas, aren't you? I'm sure it'll be wonderful.'

'Absolutely . . .' said Lucy. She paused. 'As long as he doesn't do beef. He always bloody well cooks beef, and I hate it.'

'He does love beef, it's true. As long as it doesn't have a jus. Jim finds it extremely funny that he always has a jus with everything. "All I want's a bloody shepherd's pie," he said to me last time. And that's Jim. He *never* complains.'

'Oh, the jus . . . the juices. Tell me about it, I'm sick of them,' said Lucy, entering into this with gusto. 'Gosh, we are awful.'

'We are. Just one more thing and then I'll stop,' said Florence, guiltily. 'I wish he wouldn't overload the circuits. The electrics are terrible there but he never uses the Aga, always wants everything done in a flash. He's always boiling the kettle, and you know how much electricity that uses. When we were down the other weekend there were sparks flashing out of the socket.' She blinked. 'But anyway, I'm sure it'll be lovely.'

'Oh, me too.'

They smiled at each other.

'I hope Orlando'll be OK on his own,' said Lucy after a while.

'He will,' said Florence. 'But we won't, if you're not there. You're the one who loves Christmas more than anyone else in this family. It'll be awful without you, Lucy darling. We won't have your dad this year. They've said they'll be here next year, so for the moment you have to represent your side of the family. Listen, I have a very important question. Have you wrapped your presents yet?'

Lucy smiled, and Florence thought she was trying not to cry. She reached across and squeezed her aunt's hand. 'No, not yet.'

'But it's December! I thought you were Little Miss Christmas.'

'I don't do them till the Sunday before Christmas,' said Lucy, suddenly serious. 'It's part of my Christmas routine.'

'How could I forget this?' said Florence, as the waiter brought some little shot glasses and put them down on the table with a grim flourish.

'On the house,' he said. 'Rum.'

'When in Rome drink rum,' said Lucy, clinking her glass. 'Oh, I love rum. Thank you, Flo. A family Christmas, and you with your Christmas lecture. It's lovely to see you.'

'Here's to you, darling Luce. And your wrapping, and Orlando, and everything.'

'No, no,' said Lucy, and she smiled. 'Here's to you, more like.'

'No, no. Not to either of us. Here's to Joe,' said Florence. 'Good luck, Joe.'

'To Joe,' they chorused together, smiling at each other in the gloom of the restaurant.

FLORENCE'S FAVOURITE CHRISTMAS READING

The best sitting-room at Manor Farm was a good, long, dark-panelled room with a high chimney-piece, and a capacious chimney, up which you could have driven one of the new patent cabs, wheels and all. At the upper end of the room, seated in a shady bower of holly and evergreens were the two best fiddlers, and the only harp, in all Muggleton. In all sorts of recesses, and on all kinds of brackets, stood massive old silver candlesticks with four branches each. The carpet was up, the candles burned bright, the fire blazed and crackled on the hearth, and merry voices and light-hearted laughter rang through the room. If any of the old English yeomen had turned into fairies when they died, it was just the place in which they would have held their revels.

If anything could have added to the interest of this agreeable scene, it would have been the remarkable fact of Mr Pickwick's appearing without his gaiters, for the first time within the memory of his oldest friends.

'You mean to dance?' said Wardle.

'Of course I do,' replied Mr Pickwick. 'Don't you see I am dressed for the purpose?' Mr Pickwick called attention to his speckled silk stockings, and smartly tied pumps.

'YOU in silk stockings!' exclaimed Mr Tupman, jocosely.

'And why not, sir – why not?' said Mr Pickwick, turning warmly upon him.

'Oh, of course there is no reason why you shouldn't wear them,' responded Mr Tupman.

'I imagine not, sir? I imagine not,' said Mr Pickwick, in a very peremptory tone.

Mr Tupman had contemplated a laugh, but he found it was a serious matter; so he looked grave, and said they were a pretty pattern.

'I hope they are,' said Mr Pickwick, fixing his eyes upon his friend. 'You see nothing extraordinary in the stockings, *as* stockings, I trust, sir?'

Certainly not. Oh, certainly not,' replied Mr Tupman.He walked away; and Mr Pickwick's countenance resumed its customary benign expression.

Chapter XXVIII, *A Good-Humoured Christmas Chapter*, from *The Pickwick Papers* by Charles Dickens

Martha

20 December

Martha flung down her book and stared wrathfully at nothing. From the kitchen – her kitchen – came the sound of Joe, cursing loudly about something.

She had been sitting inside all day, in the sitting room, too hot with the fire burning constantly, fidgeting because she had nothing to do. And Martha wasn't good at being idle, listening to someone else busy in her kitchen, with Cat hurrying round him, occasionally popping her head in on her grandmother.

'You all right, Gran? Another cup of tea?'

It should have been her feeding the pudding, rolling out the pastry for the mince pies, humming carols. It should have been her slicing the limes for the evening gin and tonic and opening the larder door, musing over the treasures contained therein like a dormouse, preparing for harvest. She loved the cool of the larder, stuffed full of vegetables like Harvest Festival, loved calling out for willing hands to chop and peel.

Martha chastised herself, and shifted on the hard sofa. Why did she mind so much? Joe did most of the cooking, these days. Or they hodge-podged for themselves. She was up earlier and went to bed later than ever, Cat was in and out of the house all day with the wild flowers business she was setting up, Joe's shifts were variable and they took it in turns to feed Luke and Jamie – when he was here. It was rare they sat down all together. But when they did, mostly either she or Joe shared the cooking, and it was absolutely fine. Why now, why this? Why was she so angry about being stuck here, sweltering and idle, with a stupid book about some old biddy who'd moved to the Cornish coast for her retirement and set to solving crimes. They kept offering her cups of stupid tea. She didn't want tea, she wanted . . . Martha bit her lip.

No. You said he could do it. They aren't to know, are they?

A timid knock came at the door.

'Gran . . .'

'Yes?'

'Do you want another cup of tea?'

'No thanks, Cat.'

'Joe says the preserving pan isn't big enough for the potatoes.'

'I've always found it big enough.'

Cat edged inside. 'Oh, it's so cosy in here. You look very comfortable.' She glanced awkwardly at her grandmother. 'Do you have something larger?'

'No. As I say, I usually cooked for eight to ten and it was absolutely fine.'

'But Joe says—'

It was the final straw. 'I'm off to the village,' said Martha, standing up and kicking the book under an armchair. 'I'm going to buy some limes.'

'Limes?' said Cat, bewildered. 'But, Gran, it's really cold outside. What do you need limes for?'

'Gin and tonic,' said Martha. 'I want a bloody drink, not these tepid cups of dishwater.' The thrill of her own fury made her somehow even angrier. 'And I hope it is cold. I hope it's bloody freezing. Anything's better than sitting here in this . . . in this . . . in this stupid waiting room, hanging around to die!'

She picked up her coat from the cloakroom and slammed the front door behind her.

Cat opened it, calling out to her grandmother. 'Gran! What's wrong?'

'Leave me alone!'

* * *

29

Martha stumbled out of the driveway, down the lane. The very last of the autumn leaves clung to the trees above her: the first time she had met David, they had arched overhead, a green and gold bower. Now the black branches clattered and shook in the agitated breeze, like skeletal fingers, as she walked fast, tears blinding her. She was nearly knocked down by a car on the tight bend in the road; in any event, when she reached the little bridge and the meadows below the house that led towards the village, she was crying so hard that she knew she was in no fit state to buy limes, to run the gauntlet of stares in Susan's shop. That was the trouble with village life: everyone knowing your damn business. And what a business the Winters were for them. What a business they all were.

Stopping by the bridge, and watching the swollen stream as it thundered underneath the road, Martha wiped her nose with a handkerchief, slightly calmer now. She even felt a bit silly. It was stupid, this overreaction, but she knew she was right. They had to listen to her, to understand that this was hard for her! How dare they march in and start behaving as if she were a stupid old lady who knew nothing about catering for the most important family holiday of the year. She was Martha Winter, for God's sake. She was used to providing for hordes of people: in the old days, before David died, they'd regularly have well over a hundred guests at their Christmas drinks party. Always the same date: the last Sunday before Christmas, after the Nine Lessons and Carols service at the church.

She allowed herself to think of it, just once. The house ablaze with twinkling lights, bottles of wine and Champagne thrust at odd angles outside to chill in the log pile by the front door. The two-foot-high metal pot filled with mulled wine on the Aga, and the kitchen table cleared for once, covered with little squares of smoked salmon canapés. Doors to the dining room wide open, the great mahogany dining table pushed to the side, and in the sitting room a Christmas tree as high as the ceiling next to the French windows, decorated that evening, before the carol service, by Martha and whomever else was around. No damned fire in the huge inglenook fireplace – Martha preferred cool to warmth, and besides, she'd learned long before this afternoon that roaring log fires look nice but in a room crammed with people who've dressed for warmth in an underheated church, they are unnecessary. In years gone by – when Bill, her dear pyromaniac, had been younger and more foolhardy – often there'd be a bonfire, and the younger ones would toast marshmallows and drink covert mulled wine. The grown-ups would see them through the windows, standing outside in the chill, gold-red sparks shooting up from the blaze, silver-white pinpricks of stars studding the midnight-blue sky.

She'd never really *enjoyed* those parties that much, that was the funny thing. Always work, work, work and often you were so busy you didn't get the chance to finish one drink, let alone have a proper chat to anyone. But there'd always be this moment, when she'd look around the packed, overflowing house, hear the raucous laughter, see all these people she loved so happy to be there, and Martha would feel that feeling, the one that drove her on, had driven her since the day she'd met David: this is what I have given up my career and my own dreams for. To bring people together and make them happy. To have a house full of laughter. To have a home.

And now that was all over. He was gone, and tomorrow was the last Sunday before Christmas – it was tomorrow, and there was no one who knew, no one who understood.

Most of the time she told herself she was doing rather well. That the hole left by David's absence was a visible thing. That's how she saw it, anyway: a great big black hole, waiting to swallow her up if she let it. But she'd learned to spot it when it loomed in front of her, stop and step over it, instead of falling right into it.

But lately, she couldn't stop thinking about him. This time of year he'd be singing Dean Martin and *Christmas with the Rat Pack*, practically on a loop. She sang, she knew it, all the time, but he was a beautiful singer, his light, honeyed voice crooning the old tunes to which they'd dance together in the kitchen when the children were asleep.

Martha walked on, not quite sure where to go now, sure of only one thing: she couldn't go back home just yet.

Grief was like an ocean with unpredictable tides; it came up and hit you without warning. One moment you'd be quite fine, pottering around with Cat in the garden and fussing about the sweet peas, and the next, sobbing your heart out in the greenhouse with the door shut, because of the sight of the new trowel he'd bought, a week before he died, and how he'd said the handle was tomato red, not any red, tomato red.

She might have walked past the church but the memories of the Christmas party had reminded her of the Nine Lessons and Carols service. As she looked up, Martha saw someone hurrying towards St Francis's, their arms full of greenery, and Martha remembered with a start the service was that evening. How could she have forgotten? She shook her head, miserably. She hated this – this – what was it? A mislaying of the old customs and routines that had formerly shaped her year. Things to set your watch to.

Her left knee twinged with sharp pain as she clambered off the gravelled path on to the uneven grass around the church where the headstones were, some of them centuries old, bent backwards or listing and covered with lichen. Leaning on one, she caught her breath, and looked down at David's grave. It was stark, unadorned with curlicues and quotes.

DAVID WINTER 1930–2012

'I didn't bring you anything,' Martha said, conversationally. 'I should have brought some flowers. No, some holly. Or hellebores – but there aren't any yet. Michaelmas daisies – the same. I'll bring you some snowdrops, next month. When Christmas is over . . .

I'll be back after Christmas.' She moved closer to David's grave. 'I miss you, darling,' she said, softly. 'It's soon. Do you remember it's just a few days away?'

She looked around, scratching her nose. What a stupid question to be asking. He'd been dead for two years, what did it matter who remembered what?

'Do you remember you were so late . . . and the snowdrops? Do you remember the vicar, who asked you if you were sure you wanted to go through with it? He was gay, wasn't he? He must have been.'

They'd both known he was, as he'd gone off with David's friend Ambrose after the small wedding party, held later that evening in a pub on Exmouth Market. It was just her way of comforting herself, repeating stories oft-told to each other.

'Cat's driving me up the wall,' she said, after a pause. 'She's so bossy. And Joe is useless, he's panicking. I know what he's doing wrong, and the lights buzzed this afternoon, I'm sure he's overloading the circuit. I need to sort it out, in the New Year – get on with things . . .' She stared wretchedly at the muddy, blackened winter crab grass under her feet and she said in a near-whisper, 'I don't want to be here any more without you, David. I'm sick of it. Of all of this. Of feeling like this, of being so angry and mean all the time. It's not me.' She smiled, as though he'd replied. 'Well, it's not usually this bad. Oh, David. I wish I was—'

She broke off. More footsteps behind her, crunching on the gravel. She shook her head, ashamed of herself for her melodramatics, and her eye caught the porch of the church, newly decorated with winter greenery for the service. Ivy, holly, swathes of grey-green pine, thickly set around the pointed arch of the porch. And then she heard the music – the most gentle, pulsating creak of the organ, the opening chords, the shuffle of movement.

'I'll bring you mistletoe, my darling,' she said, and she touched the gravestone gently and backed away, staring at it for a moment. And then, as if in a dream, she walked slowly towards the door of the church, and pushed it open, as the music swelled. Martha had never admitted it before but she wasn't particularly religious. But there, in the church, weary, bruised, sad beyond all help, she stood at the back and the music seemed to enter into her, like liquid gold. The hairs on the back of her neck stood up. She clutched on to the back of a pew for support.

> In the bleak midwinter,
> Frosty wind made moan.
> Earth stood hard as iron,
> Water like a stone;
> Snow had fallen, snow on snow,
> Snow on snow,
> In the bleak midwinter,
> Long ago.

At the front, Colin the choir master, and in a semi-circle, the church choir. Only the children were singing, just five of them: Kathy the vicar's children, and three others. At first the voices were soft, childish, and as she stood there watching them she realised they were beautiful.

> What can I give him,
> Poor as I am?
> If I were a shepherd,
> I would bring a lamb;
> If I were a wise man,
> I would do my part.
> Yet what I can I give him,
> Give my heart.

Give my heart. Martha wiped a tear, arms folded, swaying slightly at the sensation of the sweet, simple music. She hadn't heard music for so long. The church smelled of old mildew, wax polish, the chalky spiciness of pine. She closed her eyes, and the tears fell, coursing freely down her cheeks. One of the children – it was Sheila from the pub's grandson, she thought – looked at her curiously. Martha hurried into a pew, and sat down, so that she might carry on just listening, thinking – and crying. The choir master tapped his baton and made a few corrections, and they rustled their *Carols for Choirs* book, turning to the next page.

'Go and sit down,' said Colin. 'John will sing next.'

Up came John – a big, burly man with a beard – and he opened a copy of the *Messiah*, and the organ struck up again.

'"Comfort ye . . ."' he sang, and Martha found herself shuddering with the effort of not sobbing out loud, for David used to sing this. The *Messiah* was what they'd listened to every Christmas for years, and this was one of her favourite pieces of music. '"Comfort ye my people."'

Comfort ye. But I don't know how to, she wanted to say. I don't know how to be comforted, or to comfort.

A soft tap on her shoulder made her turn to her right, and she saw Kathy, the vicar, standing next to her.

'Room for a little one?' said Kathy.

'Of course.' Martha moved along so she could sit down. She tried to think of something normal to say. 'The choir sounds beautiful, Kathy.'

'Good. I'm so glad.' She didn't look at Martha, or touch her, just sat next to her, watching John, and smiling. 'I love the preparation for the service tonight. So much good purpose in this church. We have mince pies, shaped like Rudolph. Not strictly ecumenical, but I'll let it slide.'

Martha smiled, still watching. One of the ladies of the parish was winding ivy and pine around the wooden planks that were screwed into the choir stalls every Christmas. Another was carefully fitting thick creamy candles into each hole. In years gone by that might have been her.

'I don't like Christmas,' she said, suddenly. 'Too many memories.'

'Yes,' said Kathy easily. 'I didn't use to like it. It can be very hard, can't it?'

Slowly Martha said, 'Can I tell you something, Kathy?'

'Of course.'

'It would have been our sixtieth wedding anniversary on Christmas Eve.'

'Oh, Martha.' Kathy squeezed her hand.

Martha sat quite still, staring ahead. 'I haven't told anyone. But I can't stop thinking about it. Everyone's coming home, and they're all moving on, and they've got these wonderful new lives, and I – I want to go back in time, not forwards.' She whispered. 'I don't think I want to be alive any more, Kathy. And it's a sin, to think like that, isn't it?'

Kathy didn't move. She bowed her head and they were both silent, as the choir shuffled out of the church. Martha listened, as hard as she could. She tried to see if she could really hear something. What? David, wishing her well? But there was nothing.

After a few moments Kathy said, 'Sixty years, Martha. That's someone's life. How extraordinary that you made it to sixty years.'

'He's dead, Kathy.' Martha tried not to sound snappish.

'But you're not. You're here. You're here, right now. And your home and your family, they're here, aren't they? My father died when I was ten, did you know that?'

'No,' said Martha. 'I'm so sorry. I didn't.'

Kathy shrugged. 'It's OK. He'd been very ill for years and it was like a shadow over everything, all the time. He was a vicar, too, you see. We lived our lives around his calendar. People needed him – not just us, other people – even when he was ill. He still put others first, and that – it was really very hard. But still, that first Christmas without him . . . it was awful.' She smiled brightly. 'Yes, it really was awful. For years I hated Christmas. It seemed like a slap in the face if you were on your own, or didn't have a dad, or much money. It seemed like an excuse to point at people who weren't a "normal" family. Until I came to see we had it all wrong.'

Martha wiped her nose, and turned just a little towards Kathy. 'How do you mean?'

'Well, how do I explain it? The trouble is, we see Christmas as a holiday for those who have everything, and it's a false message. Those ads on TV – happy families walking through the snow, and all that. Whereas I see it as a holiday for those who are missing something, who want to remember that it is about a baby who was born with nothing. He was born with nothing at all, Martha, and he did great things.'

Martha shifted in her seat. 'I'm not sure I even believe in God, these days, Kathy. I'm sorry.'

Kathy shook her head, and shrugged. 'That's fine.'

'You're not going to smite me and order me from the church?'

'No,' she said, laughing. 'We'd never do that. I want you to feel welcome here whenever you want. Just think of it as a fable. A baby with nothing, born in the cold to parents with nothing, who was the one person God chose to represent us on earth. I think that's wonderful. So I think of Christmas now as a time for reflection, for remembering the small things, the ordinary people, people who are lonely and need help. That baby was one of them and he represents them all. Just a story, if you like, but I love it.' She patted Martha's arm. 'Listen some more. Stay and enjoy the music. Don't try to *be* anything – just listen. We never stop to listen. You'll hear all sorts of things, if you do.'

She put her arm around Martha and they were both silent, there in the echoing church. Martha listened again. The stillness, the warmth of Kathy's arm squeezing her, the faint scent of hymn books and Christmas, it was all beautiful. She'd never realised it before.

MARTHA'S CHRISTMAS
GINGERBREAD

Makes about 20

130g butter (half a pack)

100g dark muscovado sugar

6 tbsps golden syrup

350g plain flour

1 tsp bicarbonate of soda

3 tsps ground ginger

½ tsp cinnamon

½ tsp allspice

175g icing sugar

a little cold water

silver balls and wrapping ribbon, to decorate

Melt the butter, sugar and golden syrup in a medium saucepan. Stir until the sugar has dissolved and leave to cool for a minute or two.

Sift the flour into a bowl. Add the bicarbonate of soda, ground ginger, cinnamon and allspice. Mix into the flour.

Add the wet ingredients to the dry ingredients and stir so they form a dough. Roll into a ball. Put in the fridge wrapped in cling film for 20 minutes.

Preheat the oven to 170°C/Fan 150°/Gas 3. Flour the kitchen table. Roll out the dough to ½cm thickness. Get a medium-sized star-shaped cutter and other Christmas-appropriate shapes (nothing too small or they will burn). Cut out using cutters and place on greased or lined baking trays, not too close together. Cook for 10–12 minutes, but do check they don't catch. They should be golden brown. When still pliable and warm, pierce holes for ribbons using a skewer. Leave to cool.

Sift the icing sugar into a small bowl. Add a small amount of water to create icing the consistency of double cream. Keep adding and mixing till you get the right consistency. Pipe patterns on to the gingerbread. Decorate with silver balls on top. Thread with gold and silver wrapping ribbon and hang on the Christmas tree, on hooks in the kitchen, and anywhere in the house you like. Enjoy.

Lucy

21 December

Outside, the rain was turning to driving sleet, and the wind was picking up, but inside her East London flat Lucy Winter sat on the living-room floor, eyes alight with happiness. Three hundred and sixty-four days she'd waited for this moment. Fifty-one weeks and six days. Eleven months, three weeks and six— Well, anyway, it was here, her favourite day of the year: Christmas present wrapping day.

'Stage one,' she said aloud, and she donned the flashing reindeer antlers she'd bought in the pound shop on Kingsland High Street and which she had worn to the *Country Matters* Christmas party – she alone, amidst a sea of men in tweedy suits.

'Stage two,' she said, pulling on her new M&S bedsocks to which she treated herself, every year. The bedsocks were immensely thick, cable-knitted, with fleecy lining. They had dangling pompoms, and reindeer faces on the toes.

'Stage three.' She turned on the Bluetooth speaker and – lo and behold! – on came Michael Bublé's Christmas album, which was on a virtual loop in her flat from 25th November onwards. (Lucy had strict rules about Christmas preparations – she was obsessive enough to know she couldn't sustain this level of Christmas mania for longer than a month before the Big Day.) For a moment she tried to picture Orlando's face, were he to walk in now.

'"It's beginning to look a lot like Christmas,"' Lucy hummed. 'Yeah, Michael, I know!' she said, pretending she was on an old-style chat show with Mickey Bubbles, the two of them leaning on the piano together indulging in high-level banter. 'It sure is a wonderful time of year. How are you and your supermodel wife and baby fixed for the holidays, this year? Any plans? Hmm. Yeah, I know!' She took a photo of her feet, on the carpet, surrounded by wrapping paper, Sellotape, carrier bags of presents, and the old cardboard box of Christmas decorations she'd inherited from her dad. She posted it on Instagram.

#christmaspresentwrappingday #bestdayoftheyear

'Final stage. Stage four.' Lucy leaned forwards and removed the crystal glass with 'Baileys at Christmas' from its cardboard box, then went over to the fridge to remove the pièce de résistance: the matching flashing ice cubes and bottle of Baileys she'd been chilling for this very purpose.

The wind howled along the deserted street as Lucy raised the bottle and then stopped. She shook it repeatedly.

'Nooo,' said Lucy, softly at first, then louder. 'Nooo.' She peered inside. '*Nooooooo!*' The Baileys was all gone. 'No!' Lucy's eyes widened.

This was a Christmas ritual, as set in stone as hanging a stocking and Midnight Mass. She always wrapped her presents to either her Christmas Oldies playlist or, more recently, Mickey Bubbles' *Christmas* album, whilst drinking a Baileys in her special Baileys glass with the flashing ice cubes.

'Christmas is over!' groaned Lucy to herself dramatically, staring around the room. It was 9 p.m. and the Sainsbury's down the road would be shut. In any case, who wanted to go out in that weather? As she began wrapping the presents, sadly, the front door opened, banging loudly against the wall with the force of the wind. Lucy jumped, emitting a short, low scream. 'Orlando? That you?'

'Yes. Hello, Lucy,' said Orlando.

Orlando was one of the few people to actually *know* anything about the countryside on the staff of *Country Matters*, the glossy lifestyle magazine for people who long to live in the country but more likely are happier just flicking through pictures of golden-stone manor houses, cream teas and newborn lambs. He wrote the 'Country Folk' column and came from a long line of farmers in Worcestershire and was thus apt to chime in at editorial meetings with charming stories of owls eating their owlets or the sound a hen makes when a fox is tearing it to shreds. 'It's the reality of the countryside,' he'd say, when the girls put their hands over their eyes and started telling him to shut up.

Now he stood in the doorway by the coat rack and unwound his long thin scarf.

'How was your brother?'

'Grim,' said Orlando.

'Where did you go?'

'Some pub near Charing Cross. Absolutely stuffed full of pissed people. And us two in Barbours. Robert had a hat on. We looked a bit out of place.'

'You look out of place all the time and you live here,' Lucy pointed out. 'You don't have to wear wellies in Dalston, you know.'

Orlando looked down in some surprise at his footwear. 'But it's wet. And who cares, as long as you don't smell?'

'Words to live by,' said Lucy. 'I'm sorry, I was only teasing.'

'I like it when you tease me,' said Orlando, touchingly. 'It makes me – oh, well.' He rubbed his forehead. 'Families, eh? You're lucky, not having a brother or a sister. Trust me.'

'Oh dear. What did he do?'

'He's – well, he's a bit of a bellend.'

'Do you think you'll go back there for Christmas?'

'He's said they're not really doing Christmas, they've got too much work on with the animals. But I bet that's because his in-laws are coming instead.' Orlando pushed his glasses up his nose, and shrugged. 'To be honest, it was sort of awful last year, so it's probably for the best. It's just I miss my parents this time of year. We had beef, you know, not turkey. Dad always said it'd be rude to have anything else. Dad . . .' He trailed off, blinking hard.

'Christmas at the farm used to be so jolly. But I suppose things come to an end, don't they? I'm going to make a drink. Do you fancy something?'

'Oh.' Lucy watched him. 'Yes – I had some Baileys, but it's all gone. What do we have? I'm afraid we're all out of wine.'

Orlando put some butter in a pan. 'I'm making hot buttered rum.' He poured what seemed to Lucy to be half a foot of rum into a jug. 'Rum's good when you're feeling rubbish and you need warming up.'

'So – what will you do for Christmas?' said Lucy, softly. She wished she knew him better, that they'd lived together for years rather than just weeks so she knew the shorthand, knew what to say.

'It'll be fine, I'll stay with my aunt. She's in Stratford-upon-Avon.'

'Is she your dad's sister or—'

'My mum's. I haven't seen her for a few years but she's invited me and – oh, do you mind if we don't talk about it any more? I'm sorry, Lucy, it's not your fault, it's just Christmas always was awful after Dad died. But this year I sort of hoped my brother wouldn't be a total arse. Hey-ho.'

In the almost two months they'd lived together this was the most he'd said about anything. She knew his mother had died when he was tiny and his father at the beginning of this year, but that was it. Mostly; they talked rubbish a lot of the time. He made her laugh and it was awful, seeing him sad: Lucy's heart ached for him.

'It's the first year,' said Lucy. She put her arm around him. 'Oh, Orlando. I'm so sorry.'

Orlando added some soft brown sugar to the butter and stirred. 'It's fine.' He wrinkled his nose. 'What were you up to, anyway?'

'Wrapping presents,' Lucy said. 'But I'd run out of Baileys. You can't wrap Christmas presents without Baileys.'

Orlando beat in the rum and the spices, fast, and then took out the tiny crystal-cut tankards Lucy had inherited from her mother's mother. He poured the soft brown liquid, glinting with golden buttery flecks, into the two glasses and handed her one. 'Yes, you can,' he said. He clinked her tankard against his. 'Cheers, Lucy. And – thanks. Have a wonderful, wonderful Christmas.'

Then he leaned forwards, and kissed her. On the lips.

'Oh.' Lucy was taken aback. She could taste the butter and rum on his lips. She stared at him.

'Sorry,' said Orlando, immediately. 'Misplaced. Should have aimed to the right. Bit worse for the beer, you know. Rum on top . . . disaster.' He put his hand on her arm. 'Um . . . sorry.'

'Hey, it's Christmas,' said Lucy. 'Season of goodwill to all men, eh?'

'Yes,' said Orlando awkwardly, downing the rest of his drink. 'Look, I didn't—'

'It's fine.'

There was a silence, filled only by 'Have Yourself A Merry Little Christmas' in the background.

'Well, let me see,' said Orlando, surveying the scene as if for the first time. 'What are you doing? Can I help?'

'Sure,' said Lucy, slightly too loudly. 'Sure! Let's decorate the tree. There's some old ornaments, some new ones . . .' She crouched down by the damp and slightly worn cardboard box. 'These ones have to go on first: the golden bird, and the little girl with the hat, and the dog.'

'Why do you have a dog Christmas-tree ornament?'

She smiled. 'Dad bought one for Gran and Southpaw and one for us. He looked just like Wilbur. My grandparents' dog.'

Orlando nodded.

Every ornament taken out was like saying hello to an old friend. The rum was going down extremely well, sliding like a trail of warmth into her stomach. She brushed Orlando on the arm, as if sweeping away any awkwardness. 'It's great you're here to help. Why don't we start with this lot, then do the lights. Oh, look!' she said, with pleasure. 'The plastic eyeball! And the sheep!'

'These are the weirdest Christmas decorations I've ever seen,' complained Orlando, but he crouched down next to her. 'Where are they from?'

'My dad's,' explained Lucy. 'But he and his wife, my stepmother, they moved to Canada last year so I got them. It's my first Christmas putting them up.' She crouched down again and stared at the box. 'Strange, eh? How life changes every year, yet you cling to the old familiar things.'

'I suppose we all want to feel normal at Christmas,' said Orlando. 'But I never have. I always wonder what it'd be like if my mum was here. And I always think about, if you're Jewish, or Muslim, how strange it must be.'

'I think you can join in.'

'Sure, but perhaps you feel a bit of an outsider to begin with – and it can't help that.'

'Maybe . . .' Lucy took another sip of her drink and then gingerly set it down; her head was spinning, and she wasn't sure why. 'Maybe it should just be a winter festival. If you want to celebrate Jesus being born, that's great – but if you just want to celebrate the seasons and be with your family, that's great, too.'

'Well, of course, that's what Christmas was once,' said Orlando. 'A Winter Feast of Fools. Nothing to do with baby Jesus – wasn't he born in the summer? They'd have the Lord of Misrule and . . .' He trailed off. 'Never mind.'

'No, go on, it's really interesting.'

'You make me so nervous, that's all.' Orlando sat back on his heels, looking at her. 'I feel I have to do something when I'm around you, so I talk.'

'Oh.' Lucy stopped rummaging in the box, a delicate ornament wrapped in paper and an elastic band in her hand. 'That's – oh!' Suddenly she wished she wasn't in her onesie and bedsocks. She put the ornament on the floor and moved her hand to her head, removing the flashing antlers.

'I didn't mean to make you feel awkward,' he said, shortly. 'Now I've made it worse. I'm doing really well tonight. Rejected by my own brother, making unwanted advances towards my flatmate . . . I like you, that's all. I feel warm when you're around. Like the hot buttered rum.'

Lucy laughed, a genuine, snorting, happy laugh, and closed her eyes. Her head spun slightly.

'Do you usually laugh like that?' he asked, delighted.

'Yes,' she said, still with her eyes closed. 'Sorry, I do, yes.'

'Why have I never heard it before? It's magnificent.'

'Because I've been too shy around you. Too – silly.'

'Around *me*?' He sounded completely flabbergasted. 'Why on earth around me?'

'Orlando – oh, you lovely man. You lovely, sweet man who looks like a handsome owl man.'

'What?' he said, grinning at her. 'I think that rum's gone to your head, too.'

She put her hand on his knee.

'I fell for you the first moment I walked into the office and saw you wrestling with the printer,' she said, smiling gently at him. 'Honestly, I did.'

'*Really?*'

'Absolutely. But I thought you were too ascetic, or whatever the word is, to take a wife.' She stopped, horrified. 'I mean, not that I thought about it like that. Wives, and everything. I mean – you know.' She waved her hands. *Stop saying wife.* 'Never mind. I just mean, I always thought you were sad. And that you weren't interested in . . . in girls, or love, or romance, or anything. That's why I asked you to live with me. I knew you'd be a great flatmate, and I was so sure by then that you wouldn't . . .' She trailed off.

'That's terrible. I was so downcast when you asked me to live with you, because I knew it meant you only wanted to be friends. And I've been in love with you for months.' He was blinking at her, utterly surprised. He took her hand. 'Well. This is something of a turn-up for the books.'

His hands rested on her lap, as she sat on her knees. She reached to clasp them both – warm, sensitive long fingers, the stubby chewed nails – and kissed him again.

'Listen,' said Lucy, suddenly. 'Come to Winterfold for Christmas. I'm going tomorrow. You're off tomorrow, aren't you? Please come.'

'Isn't that a bit—'

'I'm not asking you because we've just kissed,' she said, flushing brightly. 'Only because you can't be with your aunt and your family, who are awful. Better to be alone with a good book and some telly than with them. Or with us. Really, we'd love to have you. I'll call my grandmother and check in the morning. But she'll be fine, I promise.'

Orlando rubbed his nose and poured her another glass of rum. He leaned forward and kissed her. 'Can I really come there with you? Isn't that a bit weird?'

'No, honestly, everyone's welcome there. There's always extras. Only if you promise you'll never make me eat beef,' said Lucy, seriously. 'I absolutely hate the stuff, and that's the one part of your story I have to comment on now, OK? I hate beef.'

'Well, it's just as well I've given up being a cattle farmer, then,' said Orlando.

Lucy laughed. 'Absolutely. Better throw your lot in with me. I'm going to move to the countryside and have a massive garden and two dogs and be a freelance journalist who runs a bespoke present-wrapping service on the side.' She chewed her lip. 'I'm only half-joking.'

'Brilliant. Can I come with you then, please? When are we off?'

'Tomorrow,' she said, kissing him again. 'First thing tomorrow. Tomorrow and tomorrow and more tomorrows after that.'

ORLANDO'S HOT BUTTERED RUM

Makes 1 *Thermos*

125g butter

125g soft brown sugar

500ml dark rum (not spiced rum or coconut rum – get out of here if you've got coconut-flavoured rum)

½ tsp each of cinnamon, allspice and nutmeg

a little hot water, about 50ml

Melt the butter slowly. Add the sugar and stir, taking care to mix in. Add the rum, slowly, and bring to a very gentle simmer, then add the spices. Finally, add the hot water and mix together. Leave to cool just a little.

Pour into a Thermos flask and serve around a bonfire.

Very important tip 1: Make sure the Thermos is screwed tightly on (otherwise you'll have buttery rum all over everything).

Very important tip 2: Shake well before pouring.

Winterfold

Christmas Eve

The house was built for Christmas: thick stone walls which took an age to heat up when you came back from being away but which, once warmed up, stayed that way for months. Lights twinkled outside, and through the sitting-room window the flare of the golden fire glinted on the leaded window panes.

Lucy and Luke stood with their noses pressed up against the window, looking out over the garden. The morning's hard frost had eased off a little, but upon the grass and on the bird house and the shed you could see the last of it, glinting slowly in the sinking rays of the sun. In the kitchen, *Carols from King's* rang out loudly on the radio, loud enough to be heard by them. Joe was in there, crossing Brussels sprouts, helped by Martha.

'Zach says Santa is only halfway here at the moment. Zach's dad has an app to track him on his phone. He says he's only reached Africa. He's got *ages* to go yet. What if he doesn't make it in time?' said Luke, hopping from one leg to the other.

'He'll get here,' said Lucy. 'It's Father Christmas, Luke, not Santa.'

Luke looked at her blankly. 'What?'

'Never mind. Why don't you come and help me in the kitchen?'

'No, thanks,' said Luke, extremely politely. 'I would, but I don't want to.'

'OK, well, thanks for your honesty,' said Lucy. She went into the kitchen. 'Um . . . where's Orland— Hey, Flo! When did you get here? Jim, hello! I didn't hear the car!' She kissed her aunt and Jim, Florence's partner.

Jim said, 'We parked at the top of the drive. Where's Orlando?'

49

'Yes,' said Flo. 'Where's Orlando?' She looked around eagerly.

'Subtle, guys, subtle,' said Lucy. 'I don't know where he is, actually. He disappeared after breakfast this morning. Have you seen him, Joe?'

Joe was covering the goose in oil, star anise, fennel seed and salt, rubbing the puckered skin evenly, an expression of extreme concentration wrinkling his brow. 'No. What? Don't know.'

'How about you, Gran?'

Martha looked up from her enormous earthenware bowl of greens. She topped and crossed a fresh sprout deftly without looking down. 'I don't know, darling.' She looked over towards Joe. 'Oh, the—' she began, then stopped, and sucked in her lips.

'What?' said Lucy, curiously.

'She's trying to politely tell me that I'm overloading the circuits,' said Joe, evenly. 'She's worried the electrics will blow. Because I've got the dishwasher on, as well as the Aga and the mixer and the kettle, and the lights keep flashing on and off.'

'I'm sure it's fine,' said Martha in a thin, expressionless tone. 'Right, Joe, these sprouts are done. What do you need next?'

'Nothing, thank you so much, Martha. Why don't you go—'

'And relax. I don't want to. I'd rather be kept busy.'

'No, honestly, Martha . . .' Joe swung a tea towel over his shoulder, inadvertently hitting Lucy in the eyes.

She winced, leaning forwards. 'Ow!'

'Sorry, oh shit!' Joe said, appalled. 'Lucy, are you OK?'

'It's fine—'

'I'll get the eyewash,' said Martha.

'She's fine,' said Joe, brusquely.

Cat, who had appeared in the doorway, said sharply, 'Joe! Don't talk to Gran like that!'

'I'm not talking to her like anything,' said Joe, with a weary note in his voice. He gritted his teeth. 'Can't you all, please, clear out and let me get on with it?'

'That's the problem with you, Joe,' Martha told him, wiggling her forefinger at him. 'You think cooking's a lone sport. It might be in your restaurant, but the Christmas meal isn't like that. If we don't all help then it's worthless, it's just an exercise in timed presentation skills. So tell me,' she said, and there was a terrible silence, 'what needs doing?'

'I said,' said Joe angrily, 'I don't need any help, so why don't you, all of you—'

BOOM!

A huge *phutting* spark burst out of the socket on the wall, cracking round the room, and flames shot after it. The kitchen went dark and the burglar alarm went off.

'The electrics!' Martha yelled, as Florence pulled her mother away from the Aga and the socket. 'The damned electrics, you've bloody blown them! I told you, Joe—'

'You should have had them fixed,' Joe heard himself shout above the wailing of the alarm, realising he was talking to the wall and that he couldn't see properly, as acrid smoke filled the room.

'Out,' shouted Cat, decisively. 'Everyone out! Where's Luke?'

'In the sitting room,' said Lucy. 'I'll go and get him.'

'Thanks, Luce.'

'Everyone out!' yelled Florence, rising to the occasion. 'No, Ma, no time to get a coat! Out, out, *out!*' She picked up the fire extinguisher and deftly pulled the pin. By now the flames had engulfed a wooden shelf, melting a plastic chopping board and a bag of flour, and were spreading across the counter, growing in strength with every second. Florence held the base and sprayed wildly, as Cat, standing by the door, pushed the others out, one by one.

Lucy yelled from the front of the house, 'Got Luke! Going outside!'

'*Raaaahhh!*' yelled Florence, a female Indiana Jones with an extinguisher instead of a bullwhip, as the foam covered Joe's sausage rolls, his mince pies, the crust on the beef Wellington he'd made for tonight and the goose, covered in spices and seconds away from having foil placed over it, just seconds . . .

An hour later, it was pitch-dark, and candles flickered in the kitchen as two firemen poked gingerly at the offending socket, by now a burned-out hole in the wall. Foam dripped sadly on to the floor, and Joe surveyed the scene. It was total devastation.

'Yep, this is proper burned out,' said one of the firemen. He turned to Martha. 'I'm sorry, Mrs Winter. There's no way you're having a Christmas meal in this kitchen tomorrow.' His eyes roamed the scene before him. 'We've had to turn off the Aga, as well, I'm afraid. The oil might be dangerous.'

The Aga, the source of warmth in the house, turned off: it was like taking down the sign in front of the house.

Martha nodded, shoving her hands in her pockets. She turned to Joe. 'I'm the one who should be saying sorry, Joe. Your beautiful meal is ruined.'

'What are you apologising for?' Joe said, his face half in shadow from the candles. 'I'm the one who's ruined your Christmas, your kitchen – I've wrecked the wiring, God knows how much damage it's caused.'

'Any of this salvageable?' asked Florence, picking through the dripping, foam-soaked parboiled potatoes. 'Gosh, I am sorry. I've completely ruined everything.'

'Not you, too,' said Jim, who was in the doorway.

Joe and Martha looked at each other. 'Let's blame Flo,' said Martha. 'Darling, it'd be easier if we all just agreed it was your fault. Then we can overlook that it's really our fault and we've both been behaving appallingly badly. How does that sound?'

'Fine by me,' said Florence. 'Oh dear, though, oh dear.' Her voice broke a little. 'There's absolutely nothing left.'

'Even if there was,' Martha said quietly, 'there's no way of cooking it.'

'Don't you have gas?'

'No, just the Aga, darling, and they've made us turn it off. It'll take ages to warm back up again – a day or so.'

Silence fell on the group, as foam dripped steadily on to the counters and the floor. In the darkness of the always-warm kitchen it felt as though the world had ended.

The reverie was broken by the back door swinging open and banging hard against the dresser. Joe jumped, as Cat and Luke entered, arms laden with logs from the log pile outside and with huge smiles plastered on their faces.

'Look who we found outside,' said Cat.

'Dad!' a small voice called. 'Dad! Why didn't you answer the doorbell? I've been ringing for ages, Dad!'

'Jamie?' said Joe, totally confused. He raced past the others, to the doorway, wondering if he was seeing visions in the darkness of the house. 'Jamie, son? Is that you?'

'Yes!' said Jamie, unwinding his scarf. 'I told you! I've been ringing the doorbell for ages!'

'You said you'd be—' came a voice behind him, and Joe froze. 'Oh, my God. What's happened here?'

It was his ex, Jemma, carrying a bag on her wrist and jingling some car keys. She looked around her.

'There's been an electrical fire. The power's gone off,' said Cat. 'Jemma – what are you doing here? How great to see you. I wish we could give you a proper welcome—' She dropped the logs into the basket that Joe slid over towards her feet. 'How can we make tea?' she said helplessly to Martha.

'Stoke up the fire in the sitting room,' said Martha, decisively. 'I'll look out the big old metal fireplace hanger, and we can hang the kettle and pots on that. We can boil water in no time – we can even cook pasta on it! We don't need electricity. We just need a bit of thought. Hello, Jamie,' she said, leaning down. 'It's lovely to see you, old chap.'

'Thanks,' said Jamie. ''Lo, Luke.'

'Hi, Jamie! Jamie, come and see our room, because I put a train set around the edge of the beds, and under the beds, and we can do a thing where we make the trains leap *over* the beds *comme ça*, you understand?' He mimed a fish-leaping-out-of-the-water gesture.

Jamie looked at his father in resigned despair. 'Dad,' he said, 'tell him to stop talking for a bit, eh?'

'It's fine, Jamie. But you two can't go upstairs till after the firemen have looked around. Go and help Cat in the sitting room. Scoot!' He turned to Jemma. 'I didn't know Jamie was here for Christmas?'

'I rang you three times this morning, Joe. Didn't you check your phone?'

'Not really,' said Joe. 'Reception here's rubbish, and I was working – I mean, cooking Christmas lunch.' He corrected himself before realising that was maybe why the whole enterprise had been so fraught – it wasn't work, shouldn't be work, it should be more fun than that. 'Sorry, Jemma. What's up?'

'Ian's dad's really ill,' she said. 'We have to go to Bournemouth to see him.'

'I'm so sorry. Is Ian in the car? I'll go and—'

'He's gone on ahead. Joe, I'm sorry about this. His dad's in the hospital, his mum's no good with kids. And what fun would it be for Jamie, stuck with them, when he could be at Winterfold, having the time of his life like he always does?' She looked around the kitchen, doubtfully. 'At least, that's what I thought. Perhaps—'

'No,' said Joe. 'Leave him here. Of course you should leave him here. It'd be wonderful to have him. Make my Christmas. That's all I want, to be with my boy at Christmas.' He realised how tactless that sounded, and added, 'Jemma, I'm sorry if that means—'

'Bournemouth's only an hour and a half away,' she said. 'How about if I come over on Boxing Day for lunch? Maybe Ian, too, if he thinks he can leave his dad. I don't know how long we'll be down there for.'

'What's happened?'

'Broken his leg,' she said. 'It could have been worse, but he's eighty-seven, you know. It's not great.' She smiled. 'I had such a lovely Christmas planned, too. Don't want to go on about it, because it sounds so selfish. Not with all this.'

He put his arms around her. He and Jemma had had their differences, but he'd always worked as hard as he could to have a good relationship with her. Ian, her husband, was OK, too. How awful, to have this on Christmas Eve. He kissed her hair, almost paternally. 'Chin up, kiddo. We're here if you need us, all right?'

'Sure,' said Jemma. 'What the hell are you going to do?'

Joe shook his head. 'No idea.' A grim thought crossed his mind and he looked at his watch. 'It's almost five. Shops'll be shut soon and all.' He shook his head, wanting to laugh. 'Somebody up there really wants me to fail at Christmas, I tell you.'

'So you've no Christmas dinner, no electricity, and the shops are shut.'

Cat came in again as Jemma was saying this. 'I'm sure we'll think of something,' she said. 'We can always raid the pub if necessary, Joe, can't we? Is Sheila in?'

'Of course we can. We won't starve. How many are there of us?'

Cat counted. 'Two, four, five, eight. Eight of us.'

It was then they heard Lucy, calling out from the other room. *'Orlando? Orlando, are you there?'*

'Nine,' said Cat, half-apologetically. 'I keep forgetting about him. He's a strange one, isn't he? Looks as though he's going to pull his tank top over his head and cry if you ask him a question.'

'I think he's nice,' said Joe. 'We had a good talk yesterday. He knows a lot about foraging and local customs. Grew up on a farm. Proper country boy.'

'*Orlando!*' Lucy was yelling.

'I'd better go,' said Jemma. 'You sure this is OK?' She swung her expensive bag over her shoulder. 'Can we FaceTime later?'

'Course,' said Joe. 'You want to say bye to Jamie?'

'I'll just pop through there now,' she said, and kissed Cat goodbye.

Alone in the wreckage of the kitchen, Cat put her arm around Joe's waist and kissed him. 'It'll be OK,' she murmured. 'It's only one day. We'll sort it.'

Suddenly very calm, Joe said, 'We will, won't we?'

'Yes. It doesn't matter, any of it. We're all right, Gran's cheerier, Jamie's here. It's still going to be a wonderful Christmas.'

'But what the hell are we going to actually eat?'

'There you are!' screamed Lucy.

They heard the front door creaking open. Joe made a mental note to oil it – he liked noting things about the house that needed doing, little acts of love for Winterfold that made it run smoothly as a home, this place he'd ended up in.

'Come on,' he said. 'Let's go and see what's up.'

Jemma was backing out of the drive into the darkness of the lane, as Lucy's battered old Polo zoomed down and stopped in front of the house. Orlando leaped out of it.

'Why's he driving your car?' Martha said.

'He's on the insurance. We had to drive to Scotland last month to look at a castle and – oh, it's a long story. Where have you been?' she said to Orlando. 'There was a fire, and the food's ruined, and – oh, where have you *been*?' she repeated, only in a completely different tone.

Orlando was pulling bags of Sainsbury's food out of the boot of the car. As he deposited them by the front door, he said, 'I've lived in a farmhouse most of my life, and the power always went out at some point or another. My mother always used to buy in loads of food you could cook over a fire outside just in case. She was a wise woman, my mother.'

'Orlando,' said Martha, looking at him with approval, 'you are a wonderful man.'

'Plus you had no provisions, none at all. And I didn't know what to do to be useful. I was just standing around while you all . . . um, you know . . . chopped and told each other what to do. I felt very awkward. Um . . . well, anyway. So I thought I'd just go for a bit of a spin and lay in some supplies, just in case, and if it was no good then I'd take them back to London the day after tomorrow—'

'Thin crust pizza!' shouted Luke, as he and Jamie riffled through the bags. 'Mince pies with marzipan! I love marzipan! It's the best! You bought crackers!'

'We've got crackers,' said Lucy, gazing at him in open adoration. 'The house is still standing, Orlando. You didn't need to get crackers.'

'I just thought I'd buy up what they had. And if no one needed it I'd quietly chuck it or give it away.' He shrugged. 'So . . .'

Joe walked up to him and gave him a hug. 'I love you, Orlando, you amazing man,' he said in his warm voice. 'I bloody love you.'

'I know what we can do,' said Martha, suddenly. 'Of course!'

Two hours later, they stood around a pit in the garden, hastily dug out by Joe and Jim. The embers, white as though covered with frost, glowed in the silent night and red-gold sparks spat lazily up into the sky.

They were all around it: Martha, Joe and Cat, Luke and Jamie, Lucy, Orlando, Florence and Jim, wrapped up as warmly as could be, backs freezing in the night chill and fronts burning from the heat of the fire. The grown-ups clutched hot buttered rum and sloe gin; the wine had been mulled over the fireplace hanger on the great inglenook fireplace inside and hung on a hook next to the fire pit, keeping warm.

'Pizza number one going on,' said Joe solemnly, and he slid the pizza on to the pizza stone he'd borrowed from the pub and placed gently by its handles over the fire.

Jamie and Luke squeaked with excitement: this was honestly the best Christmas ever, as far as they were concerned.

'Should take about eight minutes or so. You don't all have to wait here.'

'I like it,' said Lucy, dreamily, one hand firmly clasped in Orlando's. 'It's beautiful out here. So quiet. Look at the stars – what a clear night.'

'We might see Santa,' said Luke, urgently. 'We might see him!'

'I think you'll be in bed,' said Cat, looking back at the house, almost entirely dark except for the solar fairy lights around the Christmas tree, normally only used for the annual summer party, which had been dug out of summer storage along with the hurricane lanterns and actual lanterns that were hung in various rooms, casting a faint, golden glow. 'The electrician says he'll be here first thing on Boxing Day morning. That means no cooked food, no showers, and no heating. So we have to wrap up warm and keep the fires lit all the time – and be careful around them, you understand, boys?'

They nodded, amazed at this topsy-turvy world they were living in. 'What about TV?'

'No TV, I'm sorry.'

'The iPad?'

'It's almost out of juice, you terrible child,' said Cat. She turned to Martha, who was staring into the fire. 'It'll be OK, won't it?'

'It'll be wonderful,' said Martha. She cleared her throat. 'I want to say a few words, if that's OK.'

There was a nervous murmur of assent. She looked around them all, their faces lit golden and white in the flames. Her family, in a circle, this hotchpotch of people, so very dear to her, all of them.

'I want to raise a glass to all of you, and say how wonderful it is to have you all here. And I want to toast Joe, who I know would have made the most beautiful Christmas lunch ever, and who is a kind, lovely, truly forbearing man to put up with me, constantly telling him what to do.'

Joe looked mortified. 'Martha – no, it's not like that at all, honest.'

'Shh. It's my time to speak. I want to thank my lovely Cat, for spreading calm and good cheer, and a special thank you to my daughter Florence, for spraying every single piece of food that might have been salvageable with pressurised foam. I want to thank Jim for digging the pit, and Jamie and Luke for being our light. I want to thank Lucy for bringing this amazing man into our lives, and mostly, I want to thank Orlando, the Saviour of Christmas. To Orlando—! I don't know your surname,' she added, apologetically.

'It's Bearfleet,' said Orlando.

'Orlando Bearfleet?' said Martha, carefully. 'Goodness, you poor thing! Maybe you should change your name when you get married.'

'Gran!' hissed Lucy, as Cat cracked up.

'Orlando!' said Martha, raising her glass to him, as the fire crackled beneath them.

Orlando stared at his feet and mumbled something about how grateful he was. Lucy kissed his shoulder, blushing furiously, and they all drank deeply and looked at each other around the fire.

And then Martha said, 'I only wanted to add one more thing. David and I were married sixty years ago today. Christmas Eve, nineteen fifty-four.'

'No, Ma,' said Florence. 'I had no idea. Oh goodness, why didn't I know?'

'Oh, Gran. Really?' said Cat. 'Is that why . . .?'

'We didn't really celebrate it, what with it being Christmas Eve, and all these other things to do.' Martha nodded. 'I've been dreading today, you see. You made everything all right. Christmas is almost here, and the vicar was right. It isn't a time for those who have everything. It's best when you remember you don't need anything, except the people you love.' She cleared her throat, suddenly froggy.

In the lane below them came the sound of something moving towards them. Faint, distant voices, the crunch of boots.

'We don't need anything much, if we've got a stone to cook

pizzas on and a drink in our hands and each other, do we? What is it they say? "Let your boat of life be light."'

The carol singers from the church choir were getting louder, and as the group down by the fire pit turned they watched the figures stride into the drive and look around at the darkened house in confusion.

'We're here,' called Martha, and she strode across the frosted lawn towards them. 'Come and join us. Come!'

As she came closer, she held out her hand. Kathy was at the front of the group, and she smiled at Martha, clutching her fingers. The choir carried on singing, and Martha led them down to the fire, to the warmth of the others, the group in a circle.

It came upon the midnight clear,
That glorious song of old,
From angels bending near the earth
To touch their harps of gold:
'Peace on the earth, goodwill to men,
From heav'n's all-gracious King!'
The world in solemn stillness lay
To hear the angels sing.

They stayed there for four carols – more than any other house they'd visited – and by the end perhaps more mulled wine than is advisable had been drunk. But that was the thing about Winterfold, they all said, as they skidded back down the lane to the village. The Winters had always known how to throw a party.

Epilogue

December 1954

Clerkenwell, London

She stood outside on the steps of the church, stamping her feet and pulling at the thick winter coat she'd won at the bunfight of the jumble sale the previous week. Martha looked anxiously up at the church clock yet again.

He was never late. She was late, all the time, always the one who stood him up, who said she wasn't interested, who made out she had friends and interests far beyond him. Why was he late?

As Martha rubbed her red-raw knuckles together and blew out her breath in icy particles the vicar appeared behind her, resplendent in cassock and surplice, with a purple silken vestment over the top. He looked terrifyingly grand, like something out of a painting.

As he peered at her in the encroaching gloom, she said hurriedly, 'Father Michael, I'm sure he'll be here soon.'

'I don't doubt that you're sure of that, dear girl. I doubt whether he's coming, you see.' The vicar looked down the steps of St James's towards Clerkenwell Green. The Crown pub was busy tonight; workers were drinking their Christmas wages already, some let off early for Christmas Eve.

'He *is* coming,' said Martha, resisting the urge to stamp her foot again. She was certain of him, had been since she'd first met him, always had been.

Only yesterday, they'd rowed. She'd said she was too young to marry him, and she was having second thoughts. She wanted her career: she'd been asked to provide some drawings for an exhibition in Covent Garden. A photographer from the *Picture Post* had taken a photo of young Martha Persson, with her serious bob and her frown, sketching a portrait of Charles II in the National Gallery. The caption was: 'Young Artist Making Her Mark on Art World.' Martha's ability to imitate, to capture feeling and sentiment and not simply copy, was unusual. She had become used to thinking of herself now as someone who was good at something – not just another kid, a mouth to feed, a bum to kick, as she had been in Bermondsey.

And if she married David what would happen? Would she be churning out children like her mum, putting up with his moods, his drinking, his fists?

She laughed at her fears sometimes: David was gentle, kind, extraordinarily sweet. He would never hurt her. They wanted to build – together – a home, a life, a family.

Oh, why did I tell him no? What if he believes me? The row of the previous day, when she'd threatened to call the whole thing off, seemed to have scarred her conscious thinking: it was all she could see now, her selfishness and stupidity. And they had Christmas all planned, in the tiny one-room flat just round the corner. He'd rented it for six months in an old Clerkenwell town house, up the road from where Oliver Twist and the Artful Dodger had run amok.

Martha peered into the crowds thronging the warm, jolly-looking pub. She felt lonelier than ever – what if she'd let him get away? What would she do? Someone was singing, down the road. She listened: David loved to sing.

All I want for Christmas is my two front teeth!

This time Martha did stamp her feet, as the vicar put a consoling arm on her shoulder.

'Look, dear. Perhaps we'd better call it a night. The choir has to rehearse for Midnight Mass. We need to start. We've read the banns, dearie. You could always come back—'

Then, a little miracle.

'*I'm here!*' came a clear, loud voice, thrumming with excitement. And he was there, racing up the lane, carrying something that shook in his hand. 'I'm here, Martha! Did you think I wasn't coming?'

'Yes,' she said, running down the steps to meet him at the bottom, kissing his dear, stupid face. 'Yes, I did. Oh, David, you've no idea how sorry I am, how silly I've—'

'Darling girl! It doesn't matter.' David disentangled her frantic hands from his grasp and she saw he was holding a bunch of white flowers that smelled delicious, of perfume and musky earth. 'I had to sell a painting, and the chap at the gallery was a bleeding idiot about it. Tight as anything.' He corrected himself, nodding up at the vicar. 'Forgive me, sir.'

Father Michael, much mollified, smiled down at him. 'Already forgotten, David dear.'

'I sold it, anyway! Got three guineas for it.' He smiled at Martha, his face flushed, hair standing on end.

'David! Three guineas!'

'Yes, I did. Fella said he'd like to use me for some drawings for theatre reviews. Said he might know a chap on a newspaper.'

'Oh, David! That's wonderful!'

He pressed the snowdrops into her hands. 'I had to bring you something. These were awfully expensive, but they're worth it. Flower chap at Covent Garden said they'd come in from Holland, can you believe it? They're early snowdrops.' He kissed her.

'Snowdrops.' She hugged him again, showering his dear face with kisses, and sniffed the flowers, drinking in their delicious scent.

It had started to snow, tiny flakes almost like spots of wet paper, not proper snow, but as they looked up at the church spire in the swirling white it seemed solemn, quite right, and they joined hands and went into the church together, following the vicar.

It would snow all night and when they woke up the following day it would be silent outside, a world newly carpeted, a fresh beginning on Christmas Day.

Lightning Source UK Ltd.
Milton Keynes UK
UKOW05f2325231116
288422UK00014B/286/P

9 780993 480706